for Cuffy and Trev and Emily and Rachel and Gretchen and Alex and J.L and Stone and Hamish and Bones and Cooper and Reevsey

A Doubleday Book for Young Readers

Published by
Delacorte Press
Bantam Doubleday Dell Publishing Group, Inc.
1540 Broadway
New York, NY 10036

First published in Great Britain in 1995
by Orion Children's Books
a division of the Orion Publishing Group Ltd.
Orion House
5 Upper St. Martin's Lane
London WC2H 9EA

Doubleday and the portrayal of an anchor with a dolphin are
trademarks of Bantam Doubleday Dell Publishing Group, Inc.

Cataloging-in-Publication Data is available from the U.S. Library of Congress.
ISBN 0-385-32212-7

The text of this book is set in 24-point Garamond Light.
Book design by Tracey Cunnell
Manufactured in Italy

March 1996
10 9 8 7 6 5 4 3 2 1

Tiger the cat   Adam's grandpa   Adam's grandma   Kevin   Julie, Adam's baby-sitter   Adam Pig's dad   Tom   Angela

Adam Pig's

EVERYTHING FUN BOOK

SELINA YOUNG

A Doubleday Book
for Young Readers

the playgroup leader, Mrs. Nib   Robert   Adam's baby sister, Lisa   Adam Pig's mom   Winnie   Adam Pig   Fred the dog

These are my family and friends!

Hi! I'm Adam Pig and this is what is in my book!

Look what Adam Pig can do

he can ride his tricycle very fast!

he can pat the dog

he can paint a picture

Whoops! look at all the mess Adam's made!

he can do a puzzle

he can jump up and down

he can kick a ball

he can
look at a book

he can
touch his toes

he can
hop on one foot

he can play in his
wading pool

he can make a fort
out of blocks

he can push his wheelbarrow

I can
do all this.
What
can you do?

11

Adam Pig goes shopping

Mom was writing a shopping list. She needed apples, bread, baked beans, detergent, milk, yogurt and toilet paper.

Adam Pig looked in the cupboard. He thought Mom needed cookies, chips and fizzy drinks. Mom put the list in her bag. Then she and Adam went to the supermarket.

At the supermarket Mom got a big cart.

Adam Pig sat in the front. He held the shopping list
and Mom pushed the cart.

Mom put the things they
needed in the cart.

Adam Pig put his things
in the cart too!

When Mom had gotten all the things on the list, she pushed the cart with all the things and Adam to the checkout.

"I wonder who put these things in?" said Mom, picking up the cookies, chips and fizzy drinks. Mom said Adam could choose one thing, but the rest must go back. Adam Pig chose a fizzy drink.

Mom got out her purse and paid the lady. The lady gave Adam Pig the tape.

At home Adam helped Mom unpack the groceries.
He took out a loaf of bread, a pint of milk, one box
of detergent, two cans of baked beans, three red
apples, four rolls of toilet paper and five containers
of yogurt. Adam Pig had been so
helpful shopping that
Mom gave him one
of the red apples to
have with his
fizzy drink.
"I like shopping,"
said Adam.

Build a car with Adam Pig

a cardboard box big enough to sit in

five paper plates

scissors

paint and brushes

glue

Get a grown-up to help you cut out two door shapes in the sides of the box.

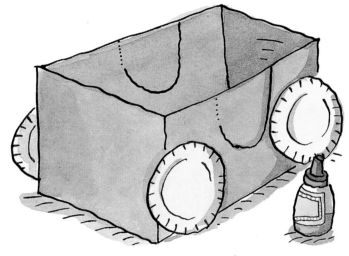

Stick on four of the paper plates to make the wheels.

Then paint the car in bright colors. Mix the paint with some glue to make it stick. Cover up any writing on the box.

Vroom vroom!

Adam Pig uses the last paper plate as a steering wheel. Now he can race off in his new car.

Adam Pig's baby sister

Adam Pig has a baby sister named Lisa. He helps Mom push Lisa in her stroller. He likes watching Lisa have her bath.

He fetches the diapers and talcum powder so Mom can change the baby.

He gives Lisa
some of his toys
to play with.
Then he
brings her
her bottle.

"What a help you are, Adam!" says Mom, and
she gives Adam Pig and Lisa a big hug.

Adam Pig goes to playgroup

Adam Pig was very excited.
It was his first day at playgroup.
Dad made him toast and jam
for breakfast. Mom helped Adam
button up his coat. Then
she took him to playgroup. She
gave him a big kiss goodbye.
Adam Pig waved to Mom
and went off with Mrs. Nib.
"This is where we hang our coats," said Mrs. Nib.
Another piglet held Adam's airplane while he hung
his coat up.

There were lots of piglets at the playgroup. They were all busy having fun. Adam soon forgot to miss his mom. Mrs. Nib showed Adam all sorts of things to do.

He painted a picture with Kevin, played dressing up with Winnie,

made a dinosaur out of blocks with Angela, and helped Robert and Tom tidy up to get ready for the story.

All the piglets sat down to hear Mrs. Nib read the story.

Afterward, Winnie and Kevin helped Mrs. Nib hand out crackers and milk.

Soon all the moms and dads started arriving to pick up their piglets. Mom came to pick Adam Pig up.

"Bye," called Adam to his new friends.

"Don't forget your painting, Adam," said Mrs. Nib.

Adam gave his painting to Mom.

"Thank you, Adam. Aren't you clever!" said Mom.

When they got home Adam helped Mom stick his painting on the fridge with four shiny magnets.

This is what you need

Print and Paint with Adam Pig

painting apron

leaves

paper

a raw potato cut into shapes

an old sponge cut into shapes

paint and paintbrushes

leaf prints

Paint your leaves in bright colors. Then press the painted leaves on the paper to get your leaf print.

potato prints

Get Mom to halve a potato and cut out a raised shape. Paint the raised shape and print it on the paper.

sponge prints

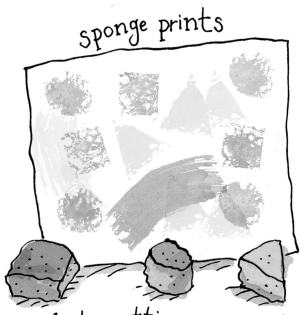

Get help cutting up an old sponge. Dip the sponge pieces in different colors. You can make lots of patterns on the paper.

Adam has used leaves, potatoes and bits of sponge to make a big picture.

Adam Pig's favorite toys

building blocks

coloring book and crayons

jack-in-the-box

boat

jigsaw puzzle

airplane

dump truck

teddy bear

What are your favorite toys?

train set

trumpet

bucket, spade and rake

robot

tool set

Adam Pig's friend

Adam Pig's
friend Kevin
had come to visit.
They were playing
with Adam Pig's
train set.

"I want to
play with the
engine," said
Kevin.

"You can't!"
said Adam.
"It's mine. I
want it!"

"Shhh! What's all this noise?" said Mom. "Why don't you build a big train with lots of cars and take turns pushing it?"

Adam Pig and Kevin made a track for their big train to go on. It was much more fun than fighting.

Adam Pig helps in the garden

Adam Pig likes visiting his grandpa. Grandpa has a big garden and there is always lots to do. Today Adam was helping Grandpa plant his vegetables.

"Spring is the best time for planting seeds," said Grandpa. First Adam Pig helped Grandpa with the digging. When the vegetable patch was ready, Grandpa made little holes for Adam Pig to put the seeds in.

They planted lettuce,
carrots, tomatoes
and beans.

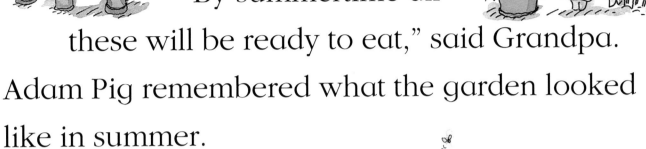

"By summertime all
these will be ready to eat," said Grandpa.
Adam Pig remembered what the garden looked
like in summer.

All the flowers were out and the sun was hot.
He would hunt for caterpillars and butterflies
and play under the sprinkler.

In autumn all the leaves
turned yellow and orange and fell
off the trees. Adam would help Grandpa to rake
them up into big piles. They were fun to play in.
In winter the snow would come and Adam and
Grandpa would wrap up warmly
and build snowpigs and
throw snowballs.

Grandma gave Adam bread crumbs to put in the bird feeder.

When Grandpa and Adam had planted all the seeds, they went inside for lunch.

"It won't be long before we'll be eating the vegetables you helped plant," said Grandpa. Adam Pig could hardly wait for summer!

Grow a bean with Adam Pig

runner bean seeds

an empty jam jar

paper towel

watering can

First soak the paper towel in water. Then put it in the jam jar.

Put one runner bean seed in the jam jar on the wet paper towel.

Make sure the paper towel stays wet. Give your bean seed a little water each day. Soon the seed will start to grow.

Look how much Adam Pig's runner bean has grown!

Adam Pig's baby-sitter

"This is Julie. She's going to baby-sit for you and Lisa while Mom and I go out," Dad told Adam Pig.

"Would you like to play a game?" asked Julie.

Adam didn't want to play any games. He wanted his mom and dad back.

"Your mom said you planted a seed in a jar," said Julie. "May I see it?"

36

Adam showed
Julie the little
shoot that had
sprouted from
his bean seed.

Then Julie read Adam and Lisa their favorite story.
Adam didn't mind having a baby-sitter at all.

Help Adam Pig get dressed

wool hat

striped top

swimming trunks

T-shirt

undershirt

shorts

underpants

bow tie

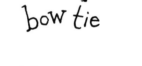
mittens

knitted vest

socks

CHEST of DRAWERS

polka-dot pants

pajamas

scarf

What shall I wear today?

coat

cardigan

pullover

sun hat

bathrobe

best suit

shirt

boots   shoes   slippers

WARDROBE

Adam Pig goes to the park

Mom helped Adam Pig put on his coat and scarf. He was going to the park.

Mom and Adam waited at the bus stop for the bus.

"Here it comes!" shouted Adam, jumping up and down. Mom bought a bus ticket. Adam Pig sat by the window. As the bus drove along he saw a spotted dog, a piglet on a bike, and a lady with lots of groceries.

Adam Pig's friends were in the park too.

"Hello, Adam," they said.

"Hello," said Adam.

Adam Pig lined up
with them to go
on the slide.

One, two, three,
whooosh!

They swung on the swings and whizzed around
and around on the merry-go-round.

Adam Pig was hot after all that whizzing!

Afterward they played hide-and-seek and tag.

"Adam," called Mom.

"It's time to go home."

"I don't want to!" said Adam.

But Mom said they had to go or they would miss the bus.

42

"Where's your scarf, Adam?" asked Mom. Oh dear! Where had Adam left it?

Adam's friends helped him look for the scarf.

Then Adam remembered he had left it on the merry-go-round. He ran over.

"Hurry!" said Mom. "Or we'll miss the bus."

Mom and Adam ran as fast as they could to the bus stop. They were just in time to catch the bus home.

This is what you need

Make a sock puppet with Adam Pig

colored felt

one old sock

scissors

glue

First get a grown-up to help you cut out two eye shapes and a tongue from the colored felt.

Glue the eyes near the toe of the sock.

Sssss!

Then turn the sock over and glue on the tongue. When the glue is dry, your puppet is ready to use.

Adam Pig calls his sock puppet Sid.

Adam Pig's favorite foods

Popsicle

cornflakes

bananas

milk

cheese

chips

watermelon

carrots

chocolate

lemonade

cookies

Jell-O

vegetable soup

spaghetti

orange juice

oranges

yogurt

pasta shapes

boiled eggs

french fries

oatmeal

fizzy drinks

raisins

crunchy apples

cheese and tomato
sandwiches

popcorn

toast and jam

waffles
with fruit

strawberries
and cream

baked potato
with cheese

**what
do you
like to eat?**

Adam Pig's birthday Party

Today was Adam Pig's birthday. He was having a party. All his friends had been sent invitations.

Adam helped Mom set the table. He helped Dad blow up the balloons. When everything was ready, Mom helped Adam into his party clothes.

Soon his friends arrived. They all had birthday
presents for Adam!
Grandpa and Grandma
arrived with an extra-
big present.

Adam sat down with all his packages.

"Thank you, everyone!"
he said when he had
opened everything.

"Let's eat," said Mom.

All the piglets sat down at the
table. There was lots to eat: sandwiches, carrot
sticks, popcorn, cherry tarts
and heaps more.

When everyone had finished, Mom brought in the cake. Dad lit the candles.

"Happy birthday to you," sang everyone to Adam Pig. Adam blew out the four candles with a big puff. Later there were party games. Adam and his friends played musical chairs, pass the present, and pin the tail on the donkey. Poor Kevin hadn't won a prize in any of the games. "Let's have another round of pass the present," said Dad.

This time Kevin won a box of colored pencils.
When it was time to go, Adam's Mom gave
everyone a slice of birthday cake to take home.
Adam's dad gave each piglet a balloon.
"Bye!" said Adam Pig.
"Thanks for having us,"
said Adam's friends as
they waved goodbye.

Adam Pig likes helping

He helps do the vacuuming

He brings the mail in

He helps brush the dog

He helps Mom to bake a cake

He helps Grandpa find his glasses

He helps feed the cat

He helps Dad wash the car

What do you do to help?

Adam Pig has chicken pox

One morning when Adam Pig woke up, he didn't feel very well. He was covered in spots!

Mom took him straight to the doctor's. The doctor looked at Adam's spots.

He listened to Adam's heart with his stethoscope. "Thump, thump," it went.

Then he took Adam's temperature. "You've got chicken pox," said the doctor. He gave Adam some cream to put on the spots.

Mom tucked Adam into bed. "You'll soon feel better," said Mom. And he did!

Adam Pig's bedtime

Adam Pig had eaten supper and was watching cartoons.

"After this one it's bathtime," said Mom.

Adam Pig liked baths, especially bubble baths.
While Mom turned on the water, Adam Pig
poured in lots of bubble bath.
"Not too much, Adam!"
said Mom.

Mom scrubbed Adam all over with a big yellow sponge. He shut his eyes tight so as not to get soap in them.

Adam played with his boats while Mom went and fetched his pajamas. She wrapped Adam up in a big fluffy towel. When he was all dry she puffed on some talcum powder. Adam hopped into his pajamas. "Don't forget to brush your teeth," said Mom. Adam squeezed lots of striped toothpaste onto his toothbrush to make sure his teeth got extra-clean.

Adam Pig was all ready for bed.
He went downstairs to say
good night to everyone.
"Night, Grandma,
night, Grandpa,
night, Lisa,
night, Dad,
night, Mom,
night, Tiger,
night, Fred."

Adam Pig wasn't tired.
"I might get sleepy if
Dad read me a story,"
said Adam.
"Just one,"
said Dad.

Adam Pig thought that one story would be fine if Mom could come up and tuck him in.

Adam picked a book for Dad to read. Mom snuggled him into bed while Dad began the story. Adam Pig was so warm and cozy that he didn't hear Dad read the last few pages. He was fast asleep.

61